In the Space of the Sky

Illustrated by
Debra Frasier

Harcourt, Inc.
San Diego   New York   London

In the Space of the Sky

of the

Sky

Richard Lewis

With thanks to my editor, Allyn Johnston,
a woman who listens with her whole heart
—D. F.

Text copyright © 2002 by Richard Lewis
Illustrations copyright © 2002 by Debra Frasier

www.harcourt.com

Library of Congress Cataloging-in-Publication Data
Lewis, Richard, 1935–
In the space of the sky/Richard Lewis; illustrated by Debra Frasier.
p.   cm.
Summary: A child's poetic view of the world—from the surrounding space
of the natural world to the inner world of dreams.
[1. Space perception—Fiction.]   I. Frasier, Debra, ill.   II. Title.
PZ7.L5877In   2002
[E]—dc21   2001001954
ISBN 0-15-253150-5

First edition
H G F E D C B A

Printed in Singapore

For Carol, with my love

—R. L.

For Rebecca,
in honor of walking
the spiraling year together.
With love and thanks

—D. F.

There—
in the
space
of the sky
is a field
for the sun,

a sea for the moon,

clouds where storms
can hide,

stars where

silence sings.

There—
in the space of the sky
are paths of birds,

rivers of air,
gardens
     of light...

growing into day,

growing into night.

There—
in the space of the
earth are hills bending,
waters gathering,
seeds opening.

Here—
a snail
curls
into
its
shell,

a bird

moves into its nest,
I go into my house.

And
there—
in the space
of my house,
I walk,
I run,
I dance,
I stand still
and wait for

another
room
to
open.

And
here—
in the
space
of my
dream,
I see
all of
the
earth
and
all of
the sky.

The collages in this book were made with Crescent and Canson papers.
The display type and text type were set in Berkely Old Style Medium.
Color separations by Bright Arts Ltd., Hong Kong
Printed and bound by Tien Wah Press, Singapore
This book was printed on totally chlorine-free Nymolla Matte Art paper.
Production supervision by Sandra Grebenar and Pascha Gerlinger
Designed by Debra Frasier and Linda Lockowitz